The Horses of the Sun Meadow
and other horse stories

Compiled by Vic Parker

Miles
Kelly

First published in 2014 by Miles Kelly Publishing Ltd
Harding's Barn, Bardfield End Green, Thaxted, Essex, CM6 3PX, UK

This edition printed 2015

4 6 8 10 9 7 5 3

Publishing Director Belinda Gallagher
Creative Director Jo Cowan
Editorial Director Rosie Neave
Senior Editor Claire Philip
Designer Rob Hale
Production Elizabeth Collins, Caroline Kelly
Reprographics Stephan Davis, Jennifer Cozens, Thom Allaway
Assets Lorraine King

ISBN 978-1-78209-455-5

Printed in China

British Library Cataloguing-in-Publication Data
A catalogue record for this book is available from the British Library

ACKNOWLEDGEMENTS
The publishers would like to thank the following artists who have contributed to this book:
Advocate Art: Simon Mendez (Cover)
The Bright Agency: Kirsteen Harris-Jones (inc. borders)
Frank Endersby

Made with paper from a sustainable forest

www.mileskelly.net
info@mileskelly.net

Contents

The Hippogriff

From *The Book of Beasts* by E Nesbit

A hippogriff is a creature that appears in myths from several different countries. It was supposed to be the offspring of a mare and a griffin – another legendary creature that had the body of a lion and the head and wings of an eagle.

LIONEL WENT DOWN INTO the library. The prime minister and the chancellor were there, and when they saw the new boy king they bowed very low, and were about to ask Lionel most politely what he was coming for when Lionel cried out, "Oh, what a worldful of books! Are they yours?"

"They are yours, Your Majesty," answered the chancellor. "They were the property of the late king, your great-great—"

"Yes, I know," Lionel interrupted. "Well, I shall read them all. I love to read. I am so glad I learned to read."

"If I might venture to advise Your Majesty," said the prime minister, "I should not read these books. Your great-great-great…"

"Yes?" said Lionel, quickly.

"He was a very good king, oh yes, really a superior king in his way, but he was a little – well, strange."

"Why?" said Lionel, puzzled.

"Well, the fact is," the chancellor explained, twisting his red beard in an agitated way, "your great…"

"Go on," said Lionel.

"…was called a wizard. And I wouldn't advise touching his books."

"Just this one," cried Lionel, laying his hands on the cover of a brown book that lay on the study table. It had gold patterns on the leather and gold clasps with turquoises and rubies in the twists of them, and gold corners.

"I must look at this one," Lionel said, for on the back in big letters he read –*The Book of Beasts*.

The chancellor sighed and said, "Don't

be a silly little king."

But Lionel had already got the gold clasps undone. He opened the first page and there was a butterfly so beautifully painted that it looked as if it were alive.

"There," said Lionel, "isn't the butterfly just lovely?"

But as he spoke the butterfly fluttered its many-coloured wings on the old page of the book, and flew up and out of the open window.

"Well!" said the prime minister. "That's magic, that is."

But the king had already turned the next page. There was a beautiful blue bird, under which was written, 'Blue Bird of Paradise', and while the king gazed enchanted at the charming picture the blue bird fluttered his wings on the page, then spread them wide and flew out of the book.

Then the prime minister snatched the book away from Lionel and shut it upon the blank page where the bird had been, and put it on a very high shelf, out of Lionel's reach.

The chancellor gave the king a good telling off, and said, "You're a naughty, disobedient little king!" He was very angry.

"I don't see that I've done any harm," said Lionel.

"No harm?" said the chancellor. "Ah, but what might have been on the next page? A snake, or something like that."

"Well, I'm sorry if I've made you cross," said Lionel. "Come, let's be friends."

So he made up with the prime minister, and they settled down for a nice quiet game of noughts and crosses while the chancellor went to add up his money.

But when Lionel was in bed he could not sleep for thinking of the book, and when the full moon was shining he got up and crept down to the library, climbed up and got *The Book of Beasts*.

He took it outside to the terrace, where the moonlight was as bright as day, and he opened the book. He saw the empty pages with 'Butterfly' and 'Blue Bird of Paradise' underneath, and then he turned onto the next page.

There was some sort of red thing sitting under a palm tree, and under it was written 'Dragon'. The dragon did not move, and the king shut up the book rather quickly and went back to bed.

But the next day he wanted another look, so he took the book out into the garden, and when he undid the clasps with the rubies and turquoises, the book opened

all by itself at the picture with dragon
underneath, and the sun shone on the page.

And then, quite suddenly, a great red
dragon came out of the book! It spread its
vast, scarlet wings and flew away across the

garden to the far hills. Lionel was left with the empty page before him.

And then Lionel felt that he had indeed gone and done it. He had not yet been king twenty-four hours, and already he had let loose a red dragon on his citizens.

Lionel began to cry. The chancellor and the prime minister and the nurse all came running to see what was the matter. And when they saw the book they understood. The prime minister and the chancellor hurried off to consult the police and see what could be done.

Everyone did what they could. They sat on committees and stood on guard, and lay in wait for the dragon, but it stayed up in the hills, and there was nothing more to be done. The faithful nurse, meanwhile, put the king to bed without any supper.

Now, the next day was Saturday. And in the afternoon the dragon suddenly swooped down upon the common in all its hideous redness, and carried off the football players, umpires, goalposts, ball and all.

The dragon stayed asleep till the following Saturday, but then it woke up with a terrible hunger and ate the prime minister and all the members of parliament.

And when the next Saturday came around, it ate an entire orphanage, before going to rest under a tree. The dragon had to go to rest under a tree or it would have caught fire from the heat of the sun. You see, the dragon was very hot to begin with and it couldn't take much more heat.

The Saturday after that, the dragon actually walked into the royal nursery and carried off the king's own pet rocking horse.

At last Lionel had an idea. He carried *The Book of Beasts* out into the rose garden, and opened it — very quickly, so that he might not be afraid and change his mind. The book fell open wide, almost in the middle, and written at the bottom of the page was the word 'Hippogriff'.

And before Lionel had time to see what the picture was, there was a fluttering of great wings and a stamping of hoofs, and a sweet, soft, friendly neighing — and out of the book came a beautiful white horse with a long white mane and a long white tail.

The Hippogriff

The horse had great wings like
a swan, and the softest, kindest eyes in the
world. It stood there among the roses, and
rubbed its silky-soft, milky white nose
against the little king's shoulder, and the

little king thought, 'But for your wings you are very like my dear lost rocking horse.' Nearby, a blue bird was singing very loudly and sweetly.

Suddenly, the king saw the great straggling, sprawling, wicked shape of the red dragon in the sky. He knew at once what he must do. He caught up *The Book of Beasts*, jumped on the back of the gentle, beautiful hippogriff, and leaning down he whispered in its white ear: "Fly, dear hippogriff, fly your very fastest to the Pebbly Waste."

And when the dragon saw them start, it turned and flew after them, with his great wings flapping like clouds at sunset.

The hippogriff's wide wings were snowy

as clouds at moonrise. And the white-winged horse flew farther and farther away, with the dragon pursuing, till he reached the very middle of the Pebbly Waste.

Now, the Pebbly Waste is just like the parts of the seaside where there is no sand – all round, loose, shifting stones, and there is no grass there and no tree within a hundred miles of it.

Lionel jumped off the white horse's back in the very middle of the Pebbly Waste, and hurriedly unclasped *The Book of Beasts*. He laid it open on the pebbles and had just jumped back onto his white horse when up came the dragon.

It was flying very feebly and looking around everywhere for a tree, for it was just on the stroke of twelve midday, the sun was shining like a gold coin in the blue sky, and there was not a tree for a hundred miles.

The white-winged horse sprang into the air and flew around and around the dragon as it writhed on the dry pebbles. It was getting very hot – indeed, parts of the dragon had even begun to smoke. It knew that it would certainly catch fire in another minute unless it could get under a tree.

The dragon made a snatch with his red claws at the king and the hippogriff, but was too feeble to reach them, and besides, it did not dare to overexert itself for fear it should get even hotter.

It was then that the dragon saw *The Book of Beasts* lying on the pebbles, open at the page with 'Dragon' written at the bottom. It looked and hesitated, and looked again, and then, with one last squirm of rage, wriggled itself back into the picture, and sat down under the palm tree. The page was a little singed as he went in.

As soon as Lionel saw that the dragon had been obliged to go and sit under its own palm tree, he jumped off his horse and shut the book with a bang.

"Oh, hurrah!" he cried. "Now we really have done it."

And he clasped the book very tightly.

"Oh, my precious hippogriff," he cried. "You are the bravest, dearest, most beautiful—"

"Hush," whispered the hippogriff

modestly. "We are not alone."

And indeed there was quite a crowd around them on the Pebbly Waste. The prime minister, the members of parliament, the football players, the children from the orphanage, the rocking horse, and indeed everyone who had been eaten by the dragon, were there. You see, it was impossible for the dragon to take them into the book, so it had to leave them outside.

And so they all went home and lived happy ever after – the hippogriff content in the greenest of green pastures.

A Horse Fair

From *Black Beauty* by Anna Sewell

As a colt, Black Beauty enjoyed a carefree life on a farm. Then he worked for a kind country squire, pulling his carriages. However, he is later bought by owners who treat him badly. After damaging his knees in an accident, he is sent to be sold at a horse fair.

NO DOUBT A HORSE FAIR is a very amusing place to those who have nothing to lose – at any rate, there is plenty to see. Long strings of young horses out of the country, fresh from the marshes, droves of shaggy little Welsh ponies, and hundreds of cart horses, some of them with their long tails braided up and tied with scarlet cord. There are a good many like myself, handsome and high-bred, but fallen into the middle class, through some accident or overwork or old age.

There were some splendid animals quite in their prime, and fit for anything. They were throwing out their legs and showing off their paces in high style, as they were trotted out with a leading rein, the groom running by the side.

But round in the background there were a number of poor things, sadly broken down with hard work, with their knees knuckling over and their hind legs swinging out at every step, and there were some very dejected-looking old horses, with the under lip hanging down and the ears lying back heavily, as if there were no more pleasure in life, and no more hope. There were some so thin you might see all their ribs, and some with old sores on their backs and hips.

These were sad sights for a horse to look upon, because one knows that one might end up in the same state.

There was a great deal of bargaining, of running up and beating down, and if a horse may speak his mind so far as he understands, I should say there were more lies told and more trickery at that horse fair than a clever man could ever give an account of.

I was put with two or three other strong, useful-looking horses, and a good many people came to look at us.

The first thing was to pull my mouth open, then to look at my eyes, then feel all the way down my legs, and give me a hard feel of the skin and flesh, and then try my paces. The difference there was in the way these things were done was wonderful.

Some did it in a rough, offhand way, as if one was only a piece of wood, while others would take their hands gently over one's body, with a pat now and then, as much as to say, "By your leave." Of course I judged a good deal of the buyers by their manners to myself.

There was one man, I thought, if he

would buy me, I should be happy. He was
not a gentleman, nor yet one of the loud,
flashy sort that call themselves so. He was
rather a small man, but well made, and
quite nimble. I knew in a moment by the
way he handled me, that he was used to
caring for horses.

He spoke gently, and his grey eye
had a cheery look in it. It may seem
strange to say, but the clean, fresh
smell there was
about him made
me take to him
– a fresh smell as

if he had just come out of a hayloft.

He offered twenty-three pounds for me, but that was refused, and he walked away. I looked after him, but he was gone, and a very hard-looking, loud-voiced man came. I was dreadfully afraid he would have me, but he walked off. One or two more came who did not mean business.

Then the hard-faced man came back again and offered twenty-three pounds. A very close bargain was being driven, for my salesman began to think he should not get all he asked, and must come down in price… but just then the grey-eyed man came back again. I could not help reaching out my head towards him. He stroked my face kindly.

"Well, old chap," he said, "I think we should suit each other. I'll give twenty-four for him."

"Say twenty-five and you shall have a deal my friend."

"Twenty-four ten," said my friend, in a very decided tone, "and not another sixpence — yes or no?"

"Done," said the salesman, "and you may depend upon it there's a great deal of quality in that horse — he's a bargain."

The money was paid on the spot, and my new master took my halter, and led me out of the fair to an inn, where he had a saddle and bridle ready.

He gave me a good feed of oats, which I very was grateful for, and he stood by while I ate it, talking to himself and talking to me.

Half an hour after we were on our way to London, through pleasant lanes and country roads, until we came into the great London thoroughfare, on which we travelled steadily, till in the twilight we reached the city.

The gas lamps were already lighted. There were streets to the right, and streets to the left, and streets crossing each other, for mile upon mile. I thought we should never come to the end of them. At last, in passing through one, we came to a long cab stand, when my rider called out in a cheery voice, "Goodnight, governor!"

"Hello!" cried a voice. "Have you got a good one?"

"I think so," replied my owner.

"I wish you luck with him."

"Thank you, governor," and he rode on. We soon turned up one of the side streets, and about halfway up that we turned into a very narrow street, with rather poor-looking houses on one side, and what seemed to be coach-houses and stables on the other.

My owner pulled up at one of the houses and whistled. Straight away the door flew open, and a young woman, followed by a little girl and boy, ran out to meet us. There was a very lively greeting as my rider dismounted.

"Now, then, Harry, my boy, open the gates, and mother will bring us the lantern."

The next minute they were all standing round me in a small stable-yard.

"Is he gentle, father?"

"Yes, Dolly, as gentle as your own kitten — come and pat him."

At once the little hand was patting about all over my shoulder without fear. How good it felt!

"Let me get him a bran mash while you

rub him down," said the mother.

"Do, Polly, it's just what he wants. And I know you've got a beautiful mash ready for my supper."

"Sausage dumpling and apple turnover!" shouted the boy, which set them all about laughing.

And then I was led into a comfortable, clean-smelling stall, with plenty of dry straw, and after a delicious supper I lay down, thinking I was going to be happy here in my new home.

The Horses of the Sun Meadow

By Andrew Lang

There are many different versions of this traditional tale, sometimes known as 'The Enchanted Knife'.

ONCE UPON A TIME there lived a young man who vowed to himself that he would only marry a royal. So one day he plucked up all his courage and went to the palace to ask the emperor for his daughter's hand in marriage. The emperor wasn't pleased at the thought of such a match for his child, so he set the lad what he thought was an impossible task. The emperor's pride and joy was his royal stable full of the fine horses — yet he had heard of three horses that were even finer still, and longed for these above all other things.

So he said, "Very well, if you can win the princess you shall have her, but these are the conditions – in eight days you must find, tame and bring to me three special wild horses. The first is pure white, the second a foxy-red with a black head, and the third is coal-black with a white head and feet. You must also bring as a present to the empress, my wife, as much gold as the three horses can carry on their backs."

The young man listened in dismay, and thought he must give in, but with an effort he thanked the emperor for his kindness and left the palace, wondering how he was to fulfil the task. Luckily for him, the emperor's daughter had overheard everything her father had said, and peeping through a curtain had seen the youth. She thought him more handsome than anyone she had ever beheld, and so she decided to help him.

She wrote him a letter and gave it to a trustworthy servant to deliver. The letter begged him to meet her early the next day.

That night, when her father was fast asleep, the emperor's daughter crept into his chamber and took out an enchanted knife from the chest where he kept his treasures.

The sun had hardly risen the following morning when the princess's maid brought the young man to meet her outside her apartments. Neither spoke for some minutes, but stood holding each other's hands. They fell instantly in love with each other, and felt full of joy.

So the emperor's daughter gave the young man the enchanted knife, which she had taken from her father.

"Take my horse," she said, "and ride straight through the wood towards the sunset till you come to a hill with three peaks. When you get there, turn first to the right and then to the left, and you will find yourself in a sun meadow, where there are many horses are feeding. Out of these many horses you must pick out the three described to you by my father. Take out this knife, and let the sun shine on it so that the whole meadow is lit up by its rays. The horses will then come to you of their own accord, and will let you lead them away.

"When you have the horses safely in

your control, find the cypress tree with brass roots, silver boughs and gold leaves. Go to it, and cut away the roots with your knife, and you will come to countless bags of gold. Load the horses with all they can carry, and return to my father, and tell him that you have done your task, and can now

claim me for your wife."

The young man did exactly as the princess instructed. The horse's were drawn to the reflection of the sun in the knife, and came willingly to him. The cypress tree was there too, just as the princess had said.

When the emperor saw the young man with the three horses he marvelled! He never guessed how the young man had outsmarted him – and he didn't realize that his enchanted knife was missing until after the wedding!